For Jeffrey, with love—I'm so happy you have chosen to ride through life with me. —S.L.

For Pauline Sobotka, exquisite equestrian and loyal friend of all creatures, two-footed and four-footed —S.J.

Published in the United States by Random House Children's Books, a division of Random House, Inc., New York. This is an adapted version of *Black Beauty* by Anna Sewell, originally published by Jarrold & Sons, London, 1877. Random House and the colophon are registered trademarks of Random House, Inc.
Visit us on the Web! www.randomhouse.com/kids. Educators and librarians, for a variety of teaching tools, visit us at www.randomhouse.com/teachers

Library of Congress Cataloging-in-Publication Data
Lerner, Sharon. Black Beauty / by Anna Sewell ; adapted by Sharon Lerner ; illustrated by Susan Jeffers. — 1st ed.
p. cm.
Summary: An illustrated adaptation for younger readers of the classic work in which a horse in nineteenth-century England recounts his experiences with both good and bad masters.
ISBN 978-0-375-85892-5 (trade) —
ISBN 978-0-375-95892-2 (lib. bdg.)
1. Horses—Juvenile fiction. [1. Horses—Fiction.]
I. Jeffers, Susan, ill. II. Sewell, Anna, 1820–1878. Black Beauty.
III. Title.
PZ10.3.L5526Bl 2009 [E]—dc22 2008033865

MANUFACTURED IN CHINA
10 9 8 7 6 5 4 3 2 1 First Edition

BLACK BEAUTY

By Anna Sewell • Adapted by Sharon Lerner
Illustrated by Susan Jeffers

Random House New York

I remember when I was just a colt. I lived in a beautiful meadow with my mother. Our master was a good and kind man, so we were very happy.

"But," my mother said, "there are many kinds of people in this world: some are kind, some are cruel, and some are just careless. I hope you will always try to be gentle and do your best to please your master or mistress."

When I was four years old, my master taught me to wear a bridle and a saddle and to carry someone on my back.

He also taught me to wear a harness and pull a carriage.

Soon after, I was sold to Squire Gordon and had to leave my mother to start my new life.

When Squire Gordon showed me to his young wife, she said, “Oh, what a beautiful horse! We shall call him Black Beauty.”

And so that became my name.

I made a lot of friends in my new home. There was a fat gray pony named Merrylegs and a handsome chestnut mare named Ginger. When I first met Ginger, she seemed angry and bad-tempered.

Squire Gordon's young daughters were afraid of her because sometimes she would bite and snap at them.

After a while Ginger and I became good friends.

She told me that the reason she seemed bad-tempered was because her former owner had treated her cruelly. It was hard for me to understand because I had only known kindness.

I was sorry for Ginger, but John Manly, our carriage man, and Joe Green, the new stable boy, were so gentle and patient with her that as weeks went by, Ginger seemed less frightened and angry.

John said, "Kindness is all the medicine she needs."

One night I was awakened by the ringing of the stable bell. "Wake up, Beauty," called John. "Our mistress is ill and we must fetch the doctor." John quickly threw on my saddle, and away we raced, through the park and down to the village.

"Mrs. Gordon is very ill," John told the doctor. "You must go to her at once." Dr. White's horse was lame, so even though I was hot and tired, I had to carry him back to the Gordon house as fast as I could.

When we got to the house, the doctor ran inside and Joe led me to the stable. I was so exhausted that I was trembling. Joe, who did not know any better, gave me cold water to drink. By the time John got home, I was lying down in my stall and shivering with cold.

John shook his head as he covered me with warm blankets. "Stupid boy," he said. "You might have killed Beauty, and he saved our mistress's life. I know it was just ignorance, but I think that is almost as bad as wickedness. People say 'I did not mean any harm' and they think that makes it all right."

I recovered quickly, but poor Mrs. Gordon was still quite ill, so the family decided to move to a warmer climate for her health.

Master Gordon sold Ginger and me to an old friend, and Merrylegs was given to the vicar.

Our new master was nice enough, but his wife liked to drive the carriage with a very tight rein to keep our heads up. It was quite painful, and finally Ginger could stand it no longer and kicked out so wildly that she fell down. That was the last time Ginger pulled the carriage.

One day Mr. York, the coachman, was away and a man named Reuben Smith was left in charge. He decided to ride me into town to the local tavern. I had a loose shoe, but Mr. Smith did not seem to notice.

On the way home he whipped me into a gallop, and my loose shoe came off on the rough cobblestones. Soon my poor hoof was broken and split. It was impossible to keep my footing on the sharp stones. I stumbled and fell to my knees.

When we were finally found and brought home, the farrier examined my knees. He said I would recover but my knees would always be scarred.

My master decided to sell me to a livery stable. I was very sad to say goodbye to Ginger.

"I am losing the only friend I ever had," said Ginger sadly as they led me away.

My new master kept many horses and carriages for hire, and because I was reliable I was greatly sought after. Many of the people who hired me didn't even know how to drive, and some thought horses were just like steam engines and tried to go as fast as they could.

But sometimes a kind person who had some driving experience hired me and that was not so bad.

One such man was Mr. Barry. He took a great liking to me and arranged to buy me as a riding horse. Unfortunately, Mr. Barry had never owned a horse before and so he hired a stable and a groom to care for me.

The groom he hired stole grain from my feed bin and was so lazy he never cleaned my stall. My feet grew sore from standing in dirty straw. Mr. Barry was disgusted and decided to give up keeping a horse. I was sold again.

This time I was sent to a horse fair, and there I was bought by a man who drove a horse cab in the city of London. His name was Jeremiah Barker but everyone called him Jerry. He brought me home to his merry family and I thought I would be happy again.

I soon learned that driving a cab through the bustling streets of the city was hard work, but Jerry gave me Sundays off to rest, so it was not so bad.

One cold winter's evening, Jerry and I drove some gentlemen to a party and we were told to wait. We stood in the freezing wind for more than two hours. Jerry had a bad cough and huddled against me for warmth. When we finally got home, Jerry's cough was so bad he could hardly speak, but he rubbed me down and put a warm blanket on me before going to bed.

The next morning no one came for me. I saw the doctor go to the house, and when the children came to feed me I realized that Jerry was very ill. The doctor said Jerry would recover but must never drive a cab again. The family was going to live in the country, where Jerry would become a coachman, and I was to be sold once more.

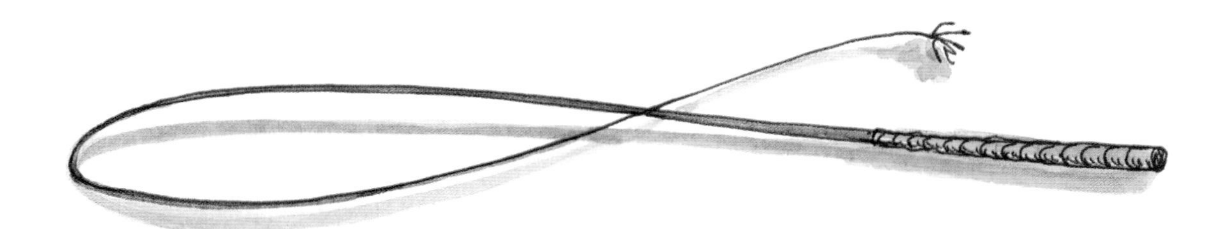

My next master was a cab driver named Nicholas Skinner. He was a cruel man and very hard on his horses. At the end of one busy day, I was carrying a family with lots of luggage and I was exhausted. When we came to a big hill, I could go no farther. Skinner used his whip on me, and when I tried to move, I slipped and fell.

As I lay on the cold ground, I heard a man say, "He's dead. He'll never get up again." Then someone put a warm blanket on me and poured water into my mouth. I slowly staggered to my feet and was led back to Skinner's stable.

After a few days of rest, I was brought to a sale for broken-down horses. Just as I was about to give up hope of ever being happy again, a young boy walked up to me and gently patted my neck.

"I like this horse, Grandpapa. Can we buy him?"

The boy's grandfather smiled as he pulled out his purse to pay for me. "You have a good eye, my boy. With some gentle care and the sweet grass in our meadows, we might begin to see the good breeding in this horse."

Mr. Thoroughgood, my new master, was as good as his word. I was given free run of a beautiful meadow and plenty of food. After several months, I began to feel young again.

One day, when it was time for me to begin work, a young man came to get me ready. As he was cleaning my face, he said, "This is just like the star Black Beauty had. I wonder where he is now?" He looked me over more carefully, and then began to smile. He was sure he knew me.

"Beauty, it's me, Little Joe Green. When I was a young stable boy and didn't know any better, I was careless and it almost killed you, but I promise I will make up for it now."

Joe kept his promise. He was the gentlest and most caring of grooms.

The young ladies of the house learned to drive me in a light cart and promised never to sell me. I was happy at last, and I was once again called by my old name, Black Beauty.